Jimmy the Racin

By M. Sterling Jones

Illustrated by Charles Snook & M. Sterling Jones

Jimmy the Racing Frog

by M. Sterling Jones & Charles Snook

Jimmy the Racing Frog

Written by M. Sterling Jones
Illustrated by Charles Snook & M. Sterling Jones

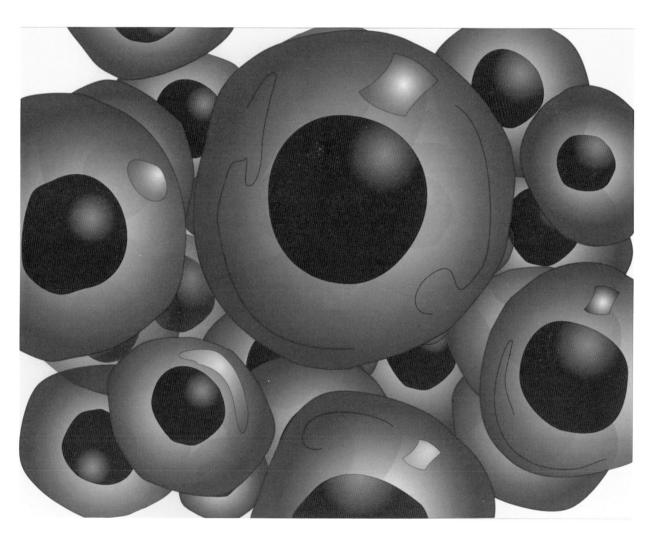

A special thanks to my wife who encouraged me to write this book and my kids who have always inspired me.

In the Beginning...5

Tadpole 9

Froglet...11

Finally a Frog...12

The Race Track..13

A New Opportunity 18

The Starling Line 20

Jimmy Finishes 23

Activities, Ideas and Education 26

by M. Sterling Jones & Charles Snook

In the Beginning

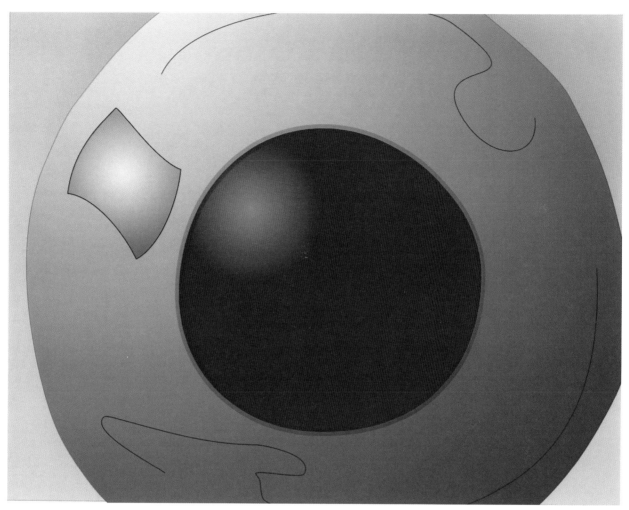

This was Jimmy as a tiny egg. He was not much bigger than a pea. His shell was a thin skin called a membrane. It wasn't hard like other eggs.

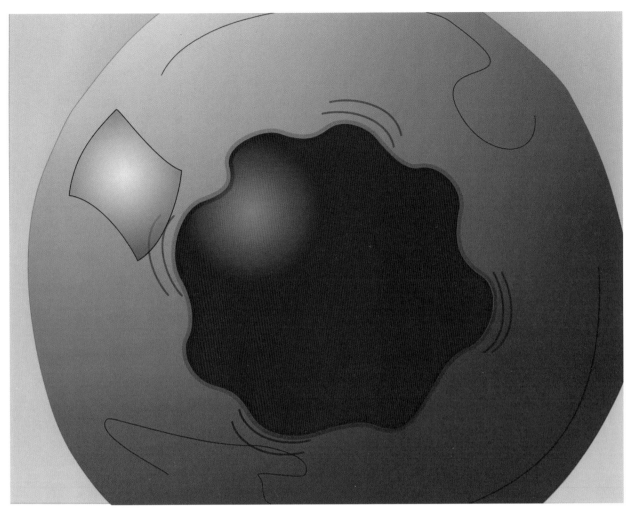

Being the main character in this story, there is something special you should know about Jimmy. Although he still didn't have any arms or legs, he had big dreams. He wanted to be a race car driver. As he grew bigger and bigger, Jimmy knew if he wanted to race cars he would have to be strong and alert. So, every morning he would wake up early and wriggle inside his egg.

Soon, he grew a tail, and every day Jimmy swished it back and forth so it would get strong. As he did he pretended he was driving his race car.

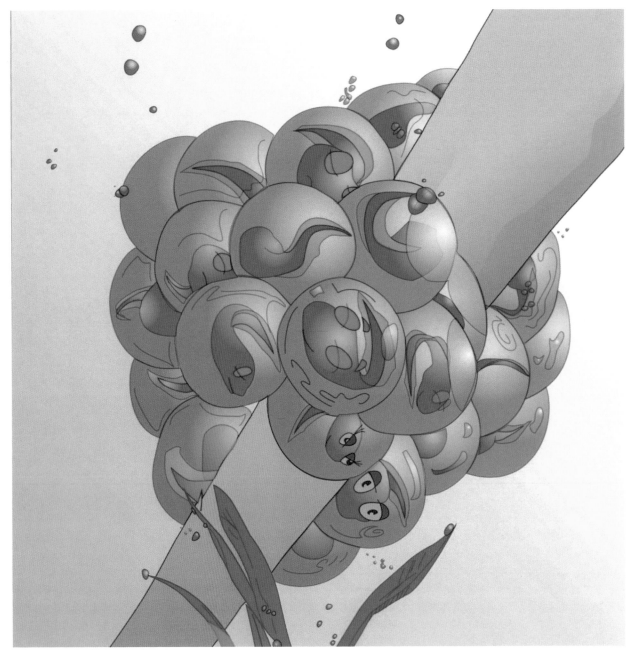

Like his 156 brothers and sisters Jimmy couldn't wait to hatch and become a tadpole.

Tadpole

A few weeks later Jimmy hatched from his egg, stretched his tail out and swam around the pond. He was a tadpole. He was so excited to be out of his egg. Every day Jimmy would pretend he was racing the other tadpoles as he swam around the pond. He would go as fast as he could, and pretty soon he was able to swim faster than the other tadpoles. Every night Jimmy dreamt of having legs to push the pedals of his car. He couldn't wait till he had them to start paddling and making them stronger.

A few weeks later his legs sprouted on either side of his tail. He kicked them hard and learned to swim even faster than before. His legs soon grew big and strong. Still, he wished that he had arms and hands to turn the steering wheel of his race car. He couldn't wait until he was a froglet.

Froglet

A few days later his arms grew in. Now Jimmy was able to crawl and pull himself out of the pond for the first time. He was finally a froglet. Every day he would go on longer and longer walks around the pond as he grew bigger and bigger. Soon he was bigger and stronger than all the other froglets in the pond.

Finally a Frog

Eventually Jimmy's tail went away. He had finally become a frog! The first day after becoming a frog, Jimmy took two big leaps down to the race track. His powerful legs had grown so big and so strong that he could jump to almost anywhere of any significance in under two leaps.

The Race Track

The track was filled with racing cars.

Frogs were everywhere getting ready to race. They were putting on helmet and fixing up or test driving their race cars. Children came from all over to watch the famous Ada County Frog Derby.

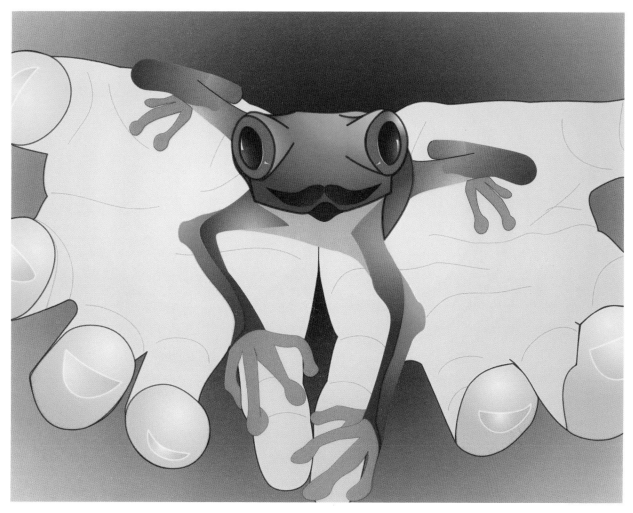

Jimmy quickly found the race track owner, who was a small tree frog from South America. He was talking to a girl named Addison who had come to watch the races. Jimmy introduced himself and excitedly told them all about his dream to race cars.

"But Jimmy, you can't be a r-r-race car driver," said the track owner in a Spanish accent. He then perched himself in Addison's hands to get a better view of Jimmy.

"Why not?" Asked Jimmy, "I can run faster and jump higher than all the other frogs in the pond. I've practiced my whole life to race cars." He looked first at the track owner then at Addison pleading for them to understand.

"Well, that's just it, Jimmy," continued the track owner. "It does take a lot of practice to be a good r-r-race car driver, but you have gr-r-rown too big."

Addison nodded in agreement.

The track owner then showed Jimmy that the cars that they use could only be driven by normal-sized frogs, whereas Jimmy was much bigger than any other frog around. All those long swims and walks around the pond had indeed made him strong. He became so big and so strong, however, that he couldn't fit into any of the race cars at the track.

Jimmy was so sad. He jumped back to the pond while the track owner and Addison watched in amazement at how far and high Jimmy could jump.

Back at the pond, Jimmy hid under some lilies and began to sob. He had practiced his whole life but now he couldn't be a race car driver.

A New Opportunity

Then Jimmy heard a girl calling his name. He slowly raised his head out of the water. It was Addison. As soon as she saw him, she ran up to the water's edge.

"Jimmy, you might not be the right size to race cars," she told the frog, "but I think you'd be the right size to be great in another sport."

"What is that?" Asked Jimmy skeptically.

"Have you ever heard of Callas County?" Asked Addison.

Jimmy shook his head.

"If you stick with me, Frog, you're going to be famous," Addison explained.

Jimmy, curious about this new opportunity, decided to not let his sadness get the best of him. He was for darn sure not going to let all his practice and hard work go to waste.

The Starling Line

The next week Jimmy entered his first competition: the Callas County Jumping Frog Championships. Every frog from Maine to California who had an inkling for jumping was welcome to enter the competition.

There were frogs of all shapes and sizes, but none were as big or as strong as Jimmy. Reporters with cameras stared up at Jimmy as he stretched his long legs. Seeing all the people and frogs who had come to watch the competition made Jimmy feel nervous.

Even worse, he wasn't used to the confined spaces, and he almost knocked over the bleachers while taking off his sweats.

Addison knelt down next to Jimmy and whispered in his ear, "Jimmy, you're the biggest and strongest frog anyone has ever seen. Now don't you fret about winning or losing. You just jump like you always do, the way you've practiced you're whole life, and you'll do fine." With that she gently patted Jimmy on the back and sat down in her spot behind him.

The announcer soon called out: "OK, jumpers to your marks…. Ready, set….. JUMP!"

In a flash the world slowed down.

Jimmy pounced higher than he ever had. Everyone watched in complete amazement as he soared high above the trees. He flew past the other contestants who were already landing after their jumps. He sailed past the crowd of children who were watching the competition and out into a vacant field.

Several seconds went by before he landed. When Jimmy looked back to see how far he'd jumped he didn't see any of the judges; they were all back near the starting line measuring for the other contestants.

Jimmy Finishes

One of the judges finally found her way down to Jimmy. After she finished measuring how far Jimmy had jumped, she called back to the announcer: "You're not going to believe this. I think we have a new world record - 175 feet 11.5 inches!"

The crowd came running. Jimmy had won! He was so thankful that he hadn't given up or let his sadness at not becoming a race car driver keep him from doing what he did best.

Addison ran up to Jimmy and scooped him up in her arms. "I knew you could do it, Jimmy. Good job."

"Thanks, " Jimmy said as he smiled and hugged Addison.

A reporter clicked his camera. The picture of a little girl hugging her friend, the Champion of Callas County, hangs to this day in the Frog Jumping Hall of Fame next to a small plaque that reads: "Because he never gave up, Jimmy is considered to be the best jumping frog in history."

THE END

Activities, Ideas and Education

1. **Using the pages that follow, draw pictures of Jimmy.**

2. **Pretend you're a frog with your brothers and sisters, or your parents.**
   - As a tadpole swimming around the pond.
   - At the Callas County Jumping Frog competition.
   - Driving a race car.

3. **Have a Origami frog jumping competition.**
Search the web and find videos that show you how to make origami jumping frogs. Then have a frog jumping competition with your friends.

4. **Education.** Search the web for site and/or articles that describe the lifecycle, habitats, and behaviors of the various species of frogs around the world.

5. **Contact Us:**
   - Author: _msterlingjones@gmail.com_
   - Illustrator: _antonysnook@gmail.com_ or _msterlingjones@gmail.com_
   - Website: _http://www.projectwoodchucks.com_.

6. **Other formats in which this book is published:**
"Jimmy the Racing Frog" is published in English on the following medium: Kindle, iBooks and paperback.

Draw Jimmy as an egg

Draw Jimmy inside his egg with a tail.

Draw Jimmy as a tadpole, hatching from his egg.

Draw Jimmy as a tadpole with legs.

Draw Jimmy as a froglet.

Draw Jimmy at the race track meeting Addison.

Draw Jimmy at the pond talking to Addison.

Draw Jimmy at the starting just before his big jump.

Draw Jimmy landing after his big jump.

Draw Jimmy hugging Addison.

Made in the USA
Lexington, KY
10 February 2012